Alumina and Kindra

Alumina and Kindra

Story and illustrations by Halline Troiani

Balboa Press books may be ordered through booksellers or by contacting:

Balboa Press
A Division of Hay House
1663 Liberty Drive
Bloomington, IN 47403
www.balboapress.com
1 (877) 407-4847

Because of the dynamic nature of the Internet, any web addresses or links contained in this book may have changed since publication and may no longer be valid. The views expressed in this work are solely those of the author and do not necessarily reflect the views of the publisher, and the publisher hereby disclaims any responsibility for them.

Any people depicted in stock imagery provided by Getty Images are models, and such images are being used for illustrative purposes only.
Certain stock imagery © Getty Images.

ISBN: 978-1-9822-0851-6 (sc)
ISBN: 978-1-9822-0852-3 (e)

Print information available on the last page.

Balboa Press rev. date: 07/18/2018

BALBOA.
PRESS
A DIVISION OF HAY HOUSE

Acknowledgements

My deepest appreciation for my family, friends, and fellow artists who helped with reading, editing, providing advice, and most of all, for your continued well wishing!

Dedication

To the child within each of us.

Winds of Change

Winds of change are blowing 'round,
Peace and harmony abound.

Sunshine streams into the breaking day,
Feel the warmth the promise in its rays.

Winds of change are blowing 'round,
Peace and harmony abound.

Whispered veils of loneliness and fear,
Fading as the waking dawn appears.

Winds of change are blowing 'round,
Peace and harmony abound.

Burning candles passing tip to tip,
Bending forward until each are lit.

As we welcome on the chain of light,
One becomes a cry of delight.

Winds of change are blowing 'round,
Peace and harmony abound.
– Halline

To Play

The snow was back. At times that was better than the rain or the heat. For although the rain was depressive, and the heat was oppressive, the cold was numbing.

Despite the snow, the urge was strong to leave. Thoughts falling, the young girl silently walked out the doorway stepping over the boundary between the den of demand, and a tousled-turf whitened by a chilly-blanket. She did not hesitate, as the sky was no bleaker than her thoughts that tried to freeze the demanding voices within the den.

Taking quick steps away she moved to the bare-bones and evergreen trail, a trail that sometimes seemed to beckon with barren fingers while repelling with thorny limbs. As she walked she felt her hurried breath becoming steady. Then, as the sun broke through the clouds, she walked into her glittering sanctuary. Here she stopped, overwhelmed by the light-embossed beauty of gracefully entwined branch, leaf and stem. The winter-greens hovering through-out with rich-brown cones and brilliant-red berries.

Momentarily entranced by the scene, a lovely sensation like a feather-tickle caused her to turn toward a tree in the clearing. Thinking she would find the usual bird, she was surprised by what looked to be a large, radiant butterfly. Watching more closely she realized the frolicking butterfly looked more like a young woman with iridescent wings. With this thought the young girl smiled, for she had always wanted to meet a fairy. She did not hesitate but walked toward the delightful looking fairy.

"You are lovely," she said as she gazed at the fairy capering around, and then as if suddenly waking up added, "and my name is Kindra."

"How thoughtful ... and I am Alumina."

Musing, Kindra lamented, "I would like to be playful, like you."

With a lighthearted smile, the fairy asked, "And why don't you play?"

"They demand I work hard, I am too silly."

"But they won't bother you here."

Pausing for a moment, Kindra's mouth melted from an icy-line to a warm-curve. Then she began to play in a stilted-hop that slowly evolved into a graceful leaping and running from rock to tree. This is when the fairy and the birds began to play along. They played until twilight descended upon the clearing.

Placidly, Kindra turned to the fairy, "Thank-you for reminding me how to let my spirit play." Alumina only smiled and waved as she flew into the deepening shadows. Reluctantly, Kindra returned to the drafty den.

To Sing

The rain was back again. Sometimes that was better than the cold or the heat. For although the rain was depressive, the cold was numbing, and the heat was oppressive.

Despite the rain, the urge was strong to leave. Thoughts drizzling, the young girl silently walked out the doorway stepping over the boundary between the den of demand, and a tousled-turf grayed by the constant cloud cover. She did not hesitate, as the sky was no grayer than her steady thoughts that tried to drown out the demanding voices within the den.

Taking quick steps away, she moved to the recently spring green and blossoming trail, a trail that sometimes seemed to beckon with leafy fingers while repelling with thorny limbs. As she walked she felt her hurried breath becoming steady. Then as the sun broke through the clouds she walked into her glistening sanctuary. Here she stopped, overwhelmed by the jewel sparkled beauty of gracefully entwined branch, leaf and stem. The varied-greens christened through-out with vibrant bud, early-flower, and pink-toned berry blossoms.

Momentarily entranced by the scene, a lovely sound, like a sonorous-scale, caused her to turn toward a tree in the clearing. Thinking she would find the usual bird, she was surprised by what looked to be a large radiant butterfly. Listening and looking more closely she realized the singing butterfly looked more like a young woman with iridescent wings. With this thought the young girl smiled for she had hoped to find the fairy. Once again, she did not hesitate but walked toward the now quiet fairy.

"Oh, that was divine," she murmured.

"How kind," lilted Alumina.

Wistfully Kindra answered, "I love to sing, too."

With an effervescent smile the fairy queried, "Why don't you sing?"

"They demand I be quiet, I am too noisy."

"But they won't hear you here."

Pausing for a moment, Kindra's mouth flashed from stormy to sunshine. Then she began to sing in a voice of whispered-longing that as she sang grew to a cheerful-boom. This is when the fairy and the birds began to sing along. They sang until twilight descended upon the clearing.

Calmly, Kindra turned to the fairy, "Thank-you for reminding me how to let my spirit sing." Alumina only smiled and waved as she flew into the deepening shadows. Resolutely, Kindra returned to the dampened-den.

To Dance

Of late, the rain had been replaced by the heat. So, although the depression had lifted with the rain, the heat was becoming oppressive.

Despite the heat, the urge was strong to leave. Thoughts kindling, the young girl silently walked out the doorway, stepping over the boundary between the den of demand, and a tousled-turf bathed in white light. She did not hesitate as the blazing sun was no worse than her glaring thoughts that tried to block out the demanding voices within the den.

Taking quick steps away, she moved to the still green and blossoming trail, the trail that sometimes seemed to beckon with unruly fingers while repelling with thorny limbs. As she walked she felt her hurried breath becoming steady. The heat of the sun was cooled by the shade of the trees as she walked into her glimmering sanctuary. Here she stopped, overwhelmed by the lustrous beauty of gracefully entwined branch, leaf and stem. The varied-greens sprayed through-out with vivid bloom, translucent petals and richly-colored berries.

Momentarily entranced by the scene, a lovely sound like swishing-silk caused her to turn toward a tree in the clearing. Thinking she would find the usual bird, she was no longer surprised by what looked to be a large radiant butterfly. Listening and looking more closely she immediately recognized the dancing butterfly who looked more like a young woman with iridescent wings. With this thought the young girl smiled for she had wanted to find the fairy. Again, she did not hesitate but walked toward the now still fairy.

"Alumina! That was wonderful."

"Kindra! How gracious."

Pausing pensive, Kindra sighed, "I love to dance, too,"

With a twinkle in her eye the fairy returned, "Why don't you dance?"

"They demand I sit still, I am too restless."

"But they won't see you here."

Pausing for a moment, Kindra's eyes flashed from hazy to sparkling. Then she began to dance with timid-hopefulness that as she moved became a dance of celebration. This is when the fairy and the birds began to dance along. They danced until twilight descended upon the clearing.

Serenely, Kindra turned to the fairy, "Thank-you for reminding me how to let my spirit dance." Alumina only smiled and waved as she flew into the deepening shadows. Deliberately, Kindra returned to the dimly-lit den.

Illumination

Snow, rain and heat were replaced with crispness and cool breezes. Weather that seemed to unthaw the senses, wake one from depression, and waft away oppression. A seasonal reflection that hinted that harvest time was near.

Despite the weather the urge to leave continued. Freedom thoughts often sent the young girl silently walking out the doorway to step over the boundary between the den of demand, and a tousled-turf now turning skeleton as colorful leaves blew off in the wind. She did not hesitate to enter the familiar terrain as it prepared for the coming season, like her steady thoughts that now could sift and soften the demanding voices within the den.

Taking quick steps away, she moved to the recently turning- to-brown and branches trail, a trail that lately, seem to beckon with naked fingers while repelling with thorny limbs. As she walked she felt her breath moving deeper. Then as the sun broke through the clouds she walked into her luminous sanctuary. Here she stopped, overwhelmed by the resplendent beauty of gracefully entwined branch, leaf and stem. The varied-greens sprinkled through-out with crisp brown, red, yellow, orange, and black-colored berries.

Momentarily entranced by the scene, the lovely sound of a familiar voice caused her to turn toward a tree in the clearing. There she found her vibrant friend, looking as always, like a large radiant butterfly. Listening and looking more closely she noticed the normally playful butterfly suddenly looked like a contemplative young woman with iridescent wings. With this thought the young girl smiled for she was blessed to know the fairy. Once, again she did not hesitate but walked toward the now intent-looking fairy.

"Alumina, you are so beautiful."

"Thank you, Kindra, and so are you."

"Thank you, I know you speak from your heart." Then Kindra asked, "But why do you look so solemn?"

With a gentle smile the fairy asked, "You have learned to play, sing and dance with your spirit?"

"Yes, I now know that I can go within my sanctuary and bring forth my spirit to join in playing, singing and dancing upon the earth."

"And if they see or hear you?"

Pausing for a moment, the young girl's face ignited with a passionate fire, "I will ask them to join me!"

Kindra then began to play, sing, and dance as her spirit rose in joyous connection with love for all that is. This is when the fairy and the birds seemed to play, sing, and dance immediately before her. Sensing a lightness, she had never before known, she glanced around her and saw the glorious wings; wings of light arching from her center outward. Lifting her upward to gaze at the delighted fairy.

Alumina spoke, "You have grown wings that can carry your spirit with-in and with-out of your illumined sanctuary."

Joyfully Kindra answered, "Thank-you for reminding me how spirit is always with me."

As twilight had fallen a golden glow had grown, Alumina smiled and waved as she flew into the moon-lit shadows. At peace, the young girl returned knowing illuminated-spirit could light the den, and perhaps one day, she would guide them to play, to sing, and to dance, and maybe; to grow wings too.

Open Your Heart

Closing down the window
Of your dreams,
Living your life perched
Between the seems,
Of sowing, what should be
And shouldn't be,
Listen to your heart you will be freed...

And, oh, peace will shine,
Oh, peace will shine,
Open your heart
And, oh, peace will shine.

You rip out stitches,
Tear your life apart,
Not knowing your own tapestry's
Fine art,
Trust rain and sun
Will flower passions seed,
Open up your heart you will be freed.

And, oh, peace will shine,
Oh, peace will shine,
Open your heart
And, oh, peace will shine.
- Halline

Winds of Change

Comporser and Lyricist: Hallline Troiani

Open Your Heart

Composer and Lyricist: Halline Troiani

Author's Biography

In pursuit of her passion for the Arts, Halline began her college career studying dance and music at a local community college. She eventually obtained a BA in Music from Cornish College of the Arts. Years later, she earned a MS in Psychology and a MA in Education. As a part of and in addition to her formal education, Halline has studied, created, performed, and taught many disciplines within the Arts, including music, dance, theater, painting/drawing, and writing.

The story of Alumina and Kindra is a collage of Halline's personal and artistic experiences expressed through story, illustration, and song. Halline has always been inspired by nature and spirituality. Having a near death experience only enhanced this inspiration, and greatly influenced her later pieces. Additionally, the experience brought an ever-present peace to her everyday life, while propelling her on a quest to learn more about alternative modes of healing and spiritual beliefs.

Halline currently live in Washington State where she loves to be outdoors. She enjoys spending time with her family, friends, cat, and two horses.

Printed in the United States
By Bookmasters